TEX
The Cowboy

1 3 5 7 9 10 8 6 4 2

This edition copyright © Sarah Garland 1995

Sarah Garland has asserted her right under the Copyright, Designs
and Patents Act, 1988 to be identified as the author and
illustrator of this work

This edition first published in the United Kingdom 1995
by The Bodley Head Children's Books
Random House, 20 Vauxhall Bridge Road, London SW1V 2SA

Random House Australia (Pty) Limited
20 Alfred Street, Milsons Point, Sydney
New South Wales 2061, Australia

Random House New Zealand Limited
18 Poland Road, Glenfield,
Auckland 10, New Zealand

Random House South Africa (Pty) Limited
PO Box 337, Bergvlei 2012, South Africa

Originally published as individual editions by
HarperCollins 1983, 1992

Random House UK Limited Reg. No. 954009

A CIP catalogue record for this book is available from the
British Library

ISBN 0 370 31851 X

Designed by Rowan Seymour

Printed in Singapore

TEX
The Cowboy

Sarah Garland

The Bodley Head
London

TEX
The Cowboy

Tex the cowboy is asleep.	The sun comes up.	Tex puts on his trousers

and his shirt and waistcoat	and his boots	and his scarf

and his gun	and his hat.	But there is one thing missing.

Tex has not got a horse.

ere is the horse market.

TEX and Gloria

Tex the cowboy goes singing down the trail.

Tex and Gloria think about food.

They see a notice on a cactus.

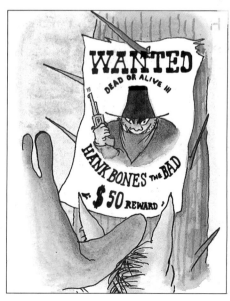

Hank leaps nimbly into the saddle

and gallops off.

At first Tex is sad.

Then he is angry.	Tex walks all day.	The sun is very hot.

But at last he finds Bad Hank Bones.		But . . .

Gloria quickly sits on Hank.

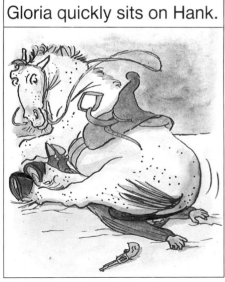

They tie Hank up and . . .

take him to the sheriff.

You are a hero, Tex

Thanks, Sheriff

Tex and Gloria have a very good dinner.

Seconds?

. . . Oh give me a home where the buffalo roam . . . .

The End

TEX
and Bad Hank

Tex and Gloria are very tired.

phew

At last they find a camp.

Fine and dandy place, Gloria

They eat their supper

and Tex sings a song.

Gloria dances

until she is quite exhausted.

All is quiet.
There is just something rustling in the bushes.

What is that something?

It is Bad Hank Bones!

Bad Hank creeps out, steals Tex's money bag and leaves instead a bag of stones.

Next morning . . .

Tex the cowboy rides into town.

Tex is having a good time . . .

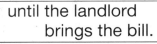

until the landlord brings the bill.

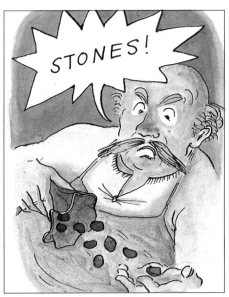

Gloria to the rescue.

TEX
The Champion

Tex and Gloria go off to get supplies

Tex is just leaving the store when . . .

Tex and Gloria have an early night

and get up in good time

to get ready for The Rodeo.

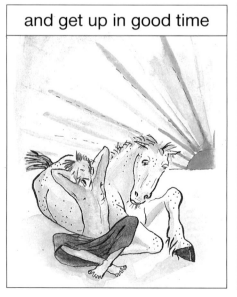

TEX
and the Hold-Up

This is the stage coach bound for Laramie.

But there is a problem.

No one will ride shotgun.

But who is this riding into town?

It is Cowboy Tex and his horse, Gloria.

They're off!

Hank has dug a pit . . .

but Gloria sees it, just in time!

Hank takes a short cut.

He climbs a tree . . .

and whirls his lasso,

But here is Gloria . . .

just in time. Again!

So, the stage coach rolls safely into Laramie.

And Tex and Gloria get their rewards!

The End

TEX
and the Gold Rush

Tex and Gloria are trying to sleep.

But there is too much noise!

Ready, steady . . .

Let's go!

They need a few things from the store.

We can spend all our money . . . .

Howdy mister

GOL SUPPL

GOLD trail

. . . because we'll soon have plenty of GOLD, Gloria!

This is the GOLD camp.

We'll soon be RICH!

GOLD CLAIMS

What a hope!

It is morning.

Tex and Gloria look up 'Gold Digging'.

First they try panning.

Then they try sieving.

Then they try hammering.

Tex is in despair.

But Gloria does not despair.

she digs . . .

and digs . . .

Until she hits an OIL well!

What dirty, disgusting water!

Let us buy a share in your OIL well, Cowboy

Please!

Please!

OIL! OIL! OIL! OIL! OIL! OIL! Please!

OIL!

Why not, pals?

This is enough GOLD for us, Gloria!

uh HUH!

The End